Varmint

and Other Tales
from the Dream World

by
India Eileen

Varmint

The scent of gasoline and rust filled the nostrils of those who stopped to transfer unleaded to their vehicles somewhere along highway 66. One hundred miles from any reputable town and the only gas station happened to be in the middle of god forsaken Arizona desert. Looking east from the rickety old gas pumps, your eyes might notice a lonely two-lane highway running between two modest towns via the middle of nowhere. North-west from the pumps sat orange tinted sand dunes and cactus-spotted hills for miles. Looking any other direction you might see the same, except south. Looking South, a stone's throw from the road, there was what looked to be a glorious mirage to the under-privileged.

A dingy little business kiosk stood about one hundred paces from where a couple bucks might get you to familiar territory. Just beyond that, as you walked deeper into the desert from the road, sat a lowly little shack and it's disjointed outhouse. With splintered wood siding and a flat rooftop, the abode stood abound ten feet tall and took up nearly forty square feet of prime desert real estate. If you were to walk in you'd be overwhelmed by the scent of tobacco ash and the sight of a hollow existence. Four lonely cots sat to the left of the crooked front door underneath a small single pane window. Somewhere in the center of the lamp lit room was a brown easy chair and a dusty rug that lingered from a time when the first proprietors sat polishing rifles or whittling small figurines. Protruding from the opposite wall there was a simple wooden counter, which was only sometimes used as a kitchen prep space. Empty bags of chips and candy bar wrappers littered the floors. What was meant for the practically non-existent patrons of the gas station kiosk replaced the nourishing meal that the two brothers who lived there didn't really know how to prepare.

The current proprietors of the establishment were Misters Joseph and Jeremiah Hatfield. They had inherited the pumps and the surrounding 14 acres from their parents about a year before.

The two never saw many people stop at their gas station, even as kids. They were both born in the shack and raised in it's solitary setting. There would be the occasional children passing through the desert with their families on vacation, but the play times would only be limited to a few minutes, if that. Mr. Hatfield was a recluse. He would wake in the morning and head straight out to mend the pumps or sit at the kiosk until dusk, downing bottles of beer and then stumbling back to his family. Mrs. Hatfield wasn't the kind of woman who anyone thought should be a mother, and she reminded her family of that every day. She was good at providing meals and threats of leaving their father, but not much more. Most of her time was spent prettying herself up and waiting around the pumps in hopes to hitch a ride to the city for a little action. One night she packed up a bag and left for good.

"Ain't nothin' goin' on around these parts. I'm bored and lookin' to live my life with someone who actually gives a damn!" She screamed at her husband one warm night while hopping in the back of some greasy passerby's Ford. Mr. Hatfield watched her hair dance in the wind as she rode off, leaving him and the boys alone for good. That night he must have decided life wasn't worth living without her there.

The next morning Joseph found his father on the kiosk porch, blood still pouring from his wrists and a short little paring knife by his side.

Young and having just made their way into adulthood, the two barely had a grasp on how to be men, with real responsibilities, let alone own a business and make a profit. There's a lot of things the heat and depletion of civilization can do to a man. The brothers learned to rely on each other the best they could, but the desert often has a way of breaking someone. Breaking them from everything they hold dear.

-

Joseph was the oldest of the two. He took on a role of leadership around the property, as well as with his younger brother, Jeremiah. There were days when he was able to sit back on his little kiosk porch around the corner, out of sight, looking beyond the deserted road running south, and just forget about his responsibilities. A lot of things weighed on Joseph, but staring out into the desert at nothing in particular, tobacco spittle filling his spittoon, well, these were the moments he looked forward to. On these warm solitary afternoons his world felt manageable and his head a little less cluttered.

Then there were days when the business or Jeremiah's youthful antics demanded more than Joseph was mentally capable of handling. Those were the days when his mind went a little darker and his sanity held on by a thread. And those days lead to uneasy nights trying to cope with what lurked outside his latched door, threatening his very existence.

-

The boys were always rambling about the property. Getting money to the gas man who refilled the tanks and the concessions kiosk once a month was the most important job the boys had to look forward to. Usually Joseph was the one to handle that business anyway. Jeremiah liked to refill the beer case because he knew Joseph always let him take one or two tall-boys if he threw a big enough fit.

The routine on that sunny summer afternoon was the same as usual. Joseph meandered from the little shaded kiosk porch where a rusted lawn chair sat next to a rusted spittoon. Handing over a wad of cash that looked, roughly, like the right amount (and often times taking a verbal lashing from Big Larry for getting the numbers wrong), Joseph paid the husky driver and then turned to check on Jeremiah.

Making his way over to his little brother, Joseph instinctively ran both hands through his hair. It was long, to his shoulders and dark brown, mostly from all the grease. Tall with the ruggedly handsome face of a movie star, he had no way of knowing that any fine young woman would fall in love with him in an instant had he ever the means to go and find one.

Jeremiah had a different look to him altogether. Blonde, slim, and toting a goofy expression with him on most days, the 16-year-old had an innocence that was ever present. It was something that Joseph, only three years older than the boy, tried to find endearing yet always thought it difficult to cope with. Because despite those times when Jeremiah was entertaining and full of youth, he had to stifle his rage at the boy for not understanding what was happening around them.

What happened at night when he slept soundly.

"It's to keep it cool around here!" Joseph heard Jeremiah explaining quite sternly in his meek southern drawl. A young woman was studying the scene while she finished filling up her caravan on pump number two.

"I still don't get it, dude." The tall brunette tugged her aviators back to her eyes from atop her head. Turning back to her vehicle, she hopped in and her music filled the natural amphitheater. With a final look at the water soaked sands around her feet she continued south, leaving a cloud of dust in her path. Joseph stopped to look at his brother, hands on his waist and a look of irritation on his face.

"Jeremiah, what the hell are you doin, boy?" He asked in a fed-up fatherly tone. Jeremiah had a hose pulled out from around the pumps and was soaking the sands surrounding the area. Blotches of darker dirt could be seen for several yards as he watched Jeremiah look down at his work. With great pride, swaying from side to side, he wore a great big grin.

"Jeremiah." Joseph said inquisitively with a small playful smile, approaching slowly, now understanding what was going on. Several empty cans of beer laid around the boy's feet. "Did you stock up those beers, boy?"

All Jeremiah could do was grin at his brother and laugh with the same coy demeanor. He started to dance about, cooing and swaying all the while, drunk on cheap Mexican beer. Joseph couldn't help but chuckle.

Before long Jeremiah had fallen in one of his soaked sand spots and blacked out. Joseph lost his grin. He meandered over to the pumps to turn off the hose's water spigot before making his way to the little hut they called home just about twenty paces away. He turned back to look at the boy, wondering if he should kick him awake and bring him inside. But he decided to wait. Or leave him. He thought about what might be the best decision, or perhaps what he could get away with, as he headed in for the night.

-

A couple of hours later Jeremiah came to.

It was dusk.

The sun had just set and the sky shone only the faintest bit of desert sun. He sat up and looked around as he rubbed his eyes. It was quiet and secluded. A feeling of peace washed over him as he soaked in the atmosphere of the home he had grown to admire. Despite all the rumor and stress in his little world, Jeremiah was a simple boy with no desire or ability to dig deeper and explain the peace he witnessed to his brother. The two held a different perspective on life, traits Jeremiah couldn't quite recognize as the handy work of their mother. His purity led him to see the little bits of beauty and little else.

After a few minutes he gathered himself with a jolt when remembering Joseph. Dusting off his khaki cover-alls he made his way the few yards back inside, all the while looking around, behind and above himself, curiously.

Jeremiah swung open the door and shut it behind him once he was inside the dimly lit shack. He looked to his brother like a puppy dog.

"I'm sorry, Joseph. I know you don't want me out there now." He said looking to the floor as he started crying, dragging his feet over to the window and drawing the curtains before landing on his shaky cot.

Joseph was standing hunched over the small bar counter opposite of Jeremiah, etching random patterns into it's surface with a small paring knife. Blood starting to boil, he stifled his anger as long as he could while wood shavings fell from the counter to his feet.

Before he could even begin scolding the boy there came a light scratching on the door that startled the tool right out of Joseph's hand. Through the little crack underneath the front door the two saw a small shadow, moving back and forth. They looked to each other with sudden pale expressions.

It was starting early tonight.

Jeremiah lowered himself to the floor slowly as Joseph grasped for his blade again in a confused state, palms becoming sweaty, eyes widened. It was quiet as he waited for the screeches and scratches. The nightly horrors of creatures climbing their way around the shack, searching for access to their own hearty meal.

Finally, the faintest cry was heard but it wasn't what was expected. A dainty *mew* echoed through the room as the two jumped and looked at each other once more. Jeremiah was quick to lower his head to the ground, looking out from underneath the door's crevasse. The half inch view showed the delicate paws of a kitten.

"Joseph, he musta saw me out there and followed me over! We gotta let him in! He'll get cold out there!" Jeremiah cried, wiping his tears away as his hand hovered over the handle, waiting for his brother's go-ahead.

Joseph hesitated but agreed.

"Make it quick then." he nodded.

Jeremiah opened the door and in ran a small gray kitten. Innocent and not yet knowing what it meant to be feral, the beast looked about the room and mewed daintily up at the two brothers. The boy scooped up the baby and held it close, petting it softly. Standing in the middle of the room, Jeremiah looked to his brother.

"I'll name him Wilbur." He said with a joyful smile. "Joseph, look! It's Wilbur!" He laughed to himself as he sat back down on the cot, the rambunctious baby purring and pawing at his new friend.

Joseph nodded assuredly, still a bit jostled from his previous assumptions of what was outside. He noticed Jeremiah hadn't closed the door and rushed the few feet over to shut it.   Taking a quick look outside, in the distance he saw them.

In the light of the moon in the now dark desert night were four or five in the pack. Claws visible from the enclosing distance, shining, from beyond the gas pumps, the creatures seemed to march together with a soldier mentality.

Swift, silent, and deadly.

To do and to endure.

They made their way towards the shack.

Not much bigger than your average sized sewer dwellers yet much hungrier, the desert rats were out.

Deathly little creatures that have been terrors since childhood, the rats had been a main source of fear for Joseph from a young age. It might have been the long claws and gleaming eyes that haunted his dreams at night. The way they run so fast toward anything that might not be able to defend itself. There are just some creatures that are stronger, wiser, more capable than others. In Africa there are tribes of ants that can eat a whole horse in a few days. Here, in this lonely desert, there are rats that can eat a man in a night.

At least that's the belief Mrs. Hatfield instilled in her two boys before up and leaving for greener pastures.

From a young age it was the topic of many a bedtime story. As she laid them to rest for the night she regaled them with stories about that one time when the poor drifter was never spotted again or how the previous residents of their home met an untimely demise. Death and terror were the result of the sounds of little feet tapping up and over their rooftop. The wildlife of the desert provided her with inspirational material that received the exact reaction that pleased her.

Whether she was merely getting her kicks with tales of fantasy or actually knew it all to be true was a mystery to Jeremiah. Joseph, however, didn't feel he could ever take the risk of not believing it. Venomous tendencies, the promise of pain and unforgettable words were the only things that his mother left him.

Slamming the door shut, Joseph turned to look at his brother who was still preoccupied with the kitten, giggling and lost in his delight. Joseph hadn't set eyes on the creatures in months. It was usually a situation where once the sun went down he'd lock up the house, put Jeremiah to bed and then fall asleep as quickly as possible while attempting to block out what screeches and scratches he knew to be lurking. Most nights he'd squirm around his cot, palms dripping sweat over his face as he covered his ears in attempt to block out the noises.

Looking around the room Joseph began hyperventilating. Grateful that his brother didn't notice his fear, Joseph began inspecting the room for weak points.

There couldn't be any weak points.

The way he saw them wobble together towards the home brought back all the emotions he felt when his mother would describe the beasts. Her voice echoed in his head as the shrieks began.

He rushed to one end of the room, eyes wide, grabbing for a pile of blankets with one hand, still absentmindedly gripping that sharp little knife in the other. B-lining for the door he fell to one knee, stuffing the material at the base of the frame. He eyed his handiwork but wasn't sure if it would be enough.

Jeremiah had meandered over to the kitchen area where he was trying to feed his kitten some scraps of food. He turned his attention, quietly, to his brother. He wearily darted glances at Joseph who paced around the room, examining the floorboards for points of access. But the scratching began. There was no time. The yelps got louder as Joseph tried to muffle the sound, bringing fists up to cover his ears, attempting to block out the tormenting sound. Soon the noise turned into heavy screaming and the tapping of claws atop the shack had gotten so loud he didn't know what to do. Why did they seem so much louder tonight? The sound resounded in Joseph's tired mind.

Jeremiah held Wilbur with care. He made his way back to his cot, deciding it wouldn't be the best night to get on Joseph's nerves. Tonight was a bad night. His big brother wasn't scared like he usually was. Joseph had anxiety attacks trying to get the boy to bed most nights; he would raise his voice or stare the boy down with daggers for eyes when Jeremiah would try to stay up late or, heaven forbid, request the two go out walking around the desert in the dark. "You don't understand what's out there, Jeremiah. You're just too simple to understand it." Joseph would chant. And Jeremiah always tried to stay out of his brother's way when he had a bad night. But sometimes it was no use.

Joseph stopped in the middle of the room. He eyed the cracks in the walls around him that revealed shadows of small bodies swiftly darting from one end of the house to the other. It was maybe one hundred rats now.

The night would only get worse and he was sure nothing could be done to further protect him and his.

Pacing about and cringing in anguish, Joseph's thoughts grew grander as he considered alternative options. What else could he do?

The sounds were deafening.

His mother's voice echoed in his head.

"It's little claws didn't seem so little as they sliced the old man's throat clean open." She would say as she vigorously tucked him into bed. He remembered her face being so long and her voice void of any sweet emotion.

Nothing he ever did eased his pain or quieted the outcry of the beasts around him.

"The blood of it's victims would spray the sands around them." He heard her say as he walked over to his brother's cot.

The words and scratching and screaming got louder. Visions of the wild rats and his father laying in a pool of blood consumed him.

Joseph felt confused and exhausted as tears began running down his cheeks. He tried so hard to make sense of the pain he had. To make it go away. But he was done trying.

"I'm not strong enough to keep going, Jeremiah" He said through hopeless sobs to his brother.

Sudden composure consumed Joseph as his mind's storm seemed to quell. There was a way to make it all stop, but only one.

He stood looking down at the blade in his hand. It was simple.

Little Wilbur jumped to the ground and ran off to the opposite corner of the room. Hunched over, hands in his lap, Jeremiah sullenly looked up at his big brother.

"It's the only way." Joseph said, a crack in his monotone voice. "I'm gonna save us from all this, brother."

In one swift motion Joseph jumped toward his brother, pulling him from the cot to the floor in the middle of the room. The two struggled as Joseph straddled his brother, locking the boy's hands under his knees and plunging the knife into Jeremiah's chest five, six, seven times. Blood sprayed Joseph's shirt and face. Confusion and darkness overtook Jeremiah as he weakly attempted to fight off his elder, engraving deep marks into the floorboards beneath him with his muddy fingernails.

Joseph proceeded the sacrifice.

"Hold still." was all he said.

When the room was no longer filled with his brother's hollow but quiet yelps, and Jeremiah stopped fighting, Joseph got to his feet. Blood continuously stained the floor around the body and Joseph studied the scene.

His bloody hand still grasped the paring knife tightly. Tugging at his soaked shirt, Joseph's eyes went from steady to weary, tears starting to roll down his cheeks. The voices were still screaming warnings at him and the sound of scratches all around him still gnawed at his soul. With continuing fear and rage he screamed like a broken warrior, taking two giant steps for the front door and throwing it open.

Despair filled the young man as he cried out to the stars, screaming again. He lifted the shining blade in the moonlight. Bringing it up to his throat he swiped it from left to right quickly before falling to his stomach on the dry sands right outside his front door. His eyes were wide and round like the moon above him as he took a final look at the still desert around him and his life faded away.

-

The desert night was quiet.

The cactus stood still and every few seconds you could hear the shifting brush in the small gusts of wind.

Suddenly, with a light rustle Wilbur exited the shack, trotting his way over Joseph's lifeless body, and onto the cool sand. He stopped to let out a lonely *mew* when he found himself face to face with a rat half his size. Wilbur hissed and backed onto his haunches. With a bat of his paw the small creature ran off.

Solitude again overcame the estate.

In the stillness of the night Wilbur walked off down the south road.

The Story of the Carpenter Ant

I was alive. It was all that mattered to me. To all of us. We lived in a town that we simply called home, among many other adjectives, good and bad. We didn't complain much and we rarely stole or hurt each other. Phrases like "capital punishment" and "throw the book" weren't really in our vocabulary. I wasn't sure of what happened to those rare few that did harm or offend others. We were relaxed. We partied sometimes. We had our city lives and our suburban family lives. Work, play, love, heartbreak, luxury and poverty played its parts. Day to day, we lived. That's all we knew, that we live right now and some day we won't. To philosophize it all was pointless and redundant to existence. That was the way of the world and we abided quietly.

To whoever may read this, well, I don't know who you are or where you come from. I don't know how you were created or what you've done with what you've been given. Your existence is a true anomaly to me but everyone, no matter where they're from, has the right to hear the story about the day the carpenter ant landed in our world and changed everything.

Me, myself, I was single and doing alright before it all happened. I kept to myself most of the time. I had a little house in a quiet neighborhood; a kitchen to enjoy my morning tea and a garden reminiscent of English setting to enjoy my sunny afternoons. I worked in the city, took the train home and lived my life with a plain, centered view on all things. I remember there was a girl that I flirted with one night while wandering around underneath the city skyline. She wore a knitted hat, had black hair, a kind face and a sultry walk that didn't seem to match her homely kind of demeanor. I was entranced and asked for her number. Unfortunately, there was little time in the days that followed to even consider the beginnings of a new romance.

It was a sunny day in Spring. Cars drove past pedestrians as they all made their way to and fro. Not a particularly special day. A weekday. The only thing that made today unique was the 300-foot-long carpenter ant that landed on the skyscrapers above us. Gasps and screams broke out within a mile as confusion began to set in. Only after a few seconds of looking to each other for answers there came another surprise as a finger, giant but perhaps accordingly proportionate to the ant itself, reached down from the blue sky and grabbed it, lifting it out of sight.

A stunned silence ensued as the populace waited for answers. As the days progressed the number of questions grew, as you could imagine. Where was the ant from? Whose hand pulled the creature away? Where was it taken to and why did it happen at all? We were a simple people, as I've described. You'd hear stories about deities and creators and things that naturally evolved into being through scientific explanation, but this was more than just a bedtime story. This was a fact. As factual as that morning cup of tea or a kiss on the cheek from your mother. It was tangent and now there was proof that something was happening beyond us and beyond our control. Who did that finger belong to and why did we just see it now?

Well, months passed as tension and opinion grew. Curiosity turned to a rage that demanded answers from the upper echelons of hierarchy who had no information to offer. Friends, family, and neighbors gathered in discussion about "higher powers" and "coincidences". Anxieties died down when the constant begging for answers became tiring, but there was still the occasional uproar. We could still walk, talk, love, but now we wondered why. We were still different colored people but who or what gave us these traits? Groups were organized in order to discuss new-found beliefs. Violence engulfed once-respectable societies, out casting those who believed in divinity versus natural order.

Eventually the rumors grew into ideas that no one knew how to deny. The grandest of them all being that this "Hand" quite literally modeled us after himself and his own world. Furthermore, he was to tear down our civilization, for we were too much for him to care for anymore.

The reason as to why differs with each person you ask but the most popular idea was that the Hand was ill and didn't have the time to watch over our world anymore, to protect us from dust or debris or carpenter ants.

So it was to happen soon.

The television was afire with "end of our world" laments and projections on when it would all go down. "This Saturday, I hear it'll be a flood, wipes us all out in a jiffy" my friend Steve, who kept up to date on the matter, had said to me. And suddenly, like wildfire, it was all anyone could talk about. The end of times will begin on Saturday.

Plans were made. Signs reading the familiar "I don't want to die a virgin! Help!" were aired on TV and the elderly found some necessity in making their last arrangements.

I wouldn't say I was skeptical but more impartial. If the world I knew *was* about to end I wanted to see some of my friends for the last time.

I had lunch on Saturday afternoon with one of my friends' family.

(And I know what you're thinking. India, the world was going to end on Saturday and you're just relaxing at lunch on the *day of apocalypse*? Well, the idea that Steve had seemed to catch on; rain. A heavy rainfall would have to occur for at least a few hours before the Hand did what he was planning to do. And if you actually let Steve sit you down and educate you on thermodynamics and weather patterns and little green men and whatnot then you'd learn something that I really couldn't articulate. Long ramblings about government seizures and conspiracy theories later, you'd have learned that during the heaviest part of the rain storm, a couple hours in, is the key time for the Hand to put our lights out. So for the rain, and Saturday night's big show, I waited.)

After the quiet lunch, Lily dropped by the house with her daughter to say a very sullen "goodbye". Then for an early dinner I went over to Steve and John's little cabin not far from my suburban home. They put the TV on and we sat around it in rickety lawn chairs in their living room, ceramic plates full of meat and potatoes on our laps, eyes glued to the news station. After dinner and a sobering broadcast, John brought out his newest contraption he wanted to show me. He said he had made it for his "last goodbye".

"What with all this rain that he's gonna drop on us...well you just touch your hand to that part there and it shocks ya till lights out. Real quick stuff." He explained.

He sat it on a table near me and we all sat for another hour or so, sharing stories and laughing as we remembered "that one time". Every now and again I'd drift off from conversation, looking over at the contraption, wondering if just one final volt would really be the best way to go. Before I could decide, the talk came to a lull and I shuffled off to the kitchen as the two huddled together in one of their last embraces. I was, surprisingly to myself, not jealous of the love they could share in these end times.

I was still alright.

When I arrived to the sink I looked down at the soap and the sponge. Not seeing a meaning to the work behind a scrubbed dish today, I sat them down and peered calmly out of the little window. Homes, roads, and trees that once stood in place were absent. It seemed the theory of doom by rain had been misplaced. I didn't understand how it was all happening but I couldn't believe my eyes, as it was all true. There was nothing we could do but wait. As I kept looking at my new blank surroundings I couldn't help but notice a neighboring man outside chopping down trees with a chainsaw. He had a lazy manor about the job, in a very haphazard way. I was torn between wonder and concern at why he thought any of this mattered. I opened the window and yelled to him.

"Why are you chopping down trees?" I asked.

He turned to me with a calm face and very tired eyes. "I really can't say." He responded as if he had suffered some harassment surrounding the topic all day. Tears filled his eyes and he stopped to really look at his progress. He looked back at me and all I could offer was a nod and a half grin. I felt hopeless. I felt raw and numb and as if nothing I could say would matter to anyone, even myself.

I sensed my death for the first time.

I turned back to where my friends sat, explaining that I enjoyed the company but I had to leave. They understood and I showed myself out.

Back in my kitchen the sun was beginning to set. I stood looking at the things I owned and remembering all the emotions it evoked inside me, wondering if any of my aspirations meant anything at all. I sat on the floor for a while, considering the future or lack thereof. Dusk arrived and I stood to look out the window. All of my neighbors, all of their finely trimmed topiaries and their yappy dogs and their paved driveways were no more. It was a sage green ground that cut into a grey, foggy sky as far as the eye could see. If they were gone I must be next.

My kitchen was barely lit and as I turned to look around it one last time I noticed that many of my things had disappeared except for a dusty old cake pan and a single rose in a vase I had placed in the windowsill that morning. Picking up the pan, I watched my rose as I worked in slow circular motions with my sleeve to dust off the tin. Since the Hand appeared in our world everything was less serious to me. I felt calm and ready for the physical change I was about to feel. Still, curiosity ensued with every passing second.

I lowered myself to the kitchen floor once more. My hands shook. I placed the pan back on the counter as my knees met the cold tile. I guess, in my mind, it was just time to sit and wait for what I felt was about to happen. And then suddenly, yet so wonderfully, it did. I couldn't believe it. I was stunned by the beauty of what my body felt in that moment.

My breath began to fail me and I was almost too excited. Happy. I looked around the room only to notice the rose in my hand. As my head grew lighter I saw the flower shrivel to a blackened corpse, melting to the floor from my grasp. I grabbed for my chest as I mouthed the words "here it is" and fell to my side. Grabbing and tugging at my shirt, I smiled. It was happening so quickly that just as I had lived my life with little worry, I was leaving it with the same disposition. Dizziness consumed me and the natural high was overwhelming. The pressure was low. I was fading fast and with a last thought I was taken away.

"And...I'm dying." I thought.

"And...I'm dead."

A Case of Mistaken Identity

For her own reasons it was important that Georgia took the risk, followed her gut, and made sure everything was on the up and up. Finding more out about Steve seemed important. Who did he think she was? What did he know about Isabelle? The woman was going to find all the answers and if she happened to get a thrill in the meantime then so be it.

Georgia

Sometimes it was all the young woman could do to keep from screaming "girl power" themed obscenities at her coworkers on a daily basis. Jokes and slights at her way of life, they were all in good fun, she was sure. It's not like anyone actually resented her for living out of a van, or even hated her for it. Why would they? A few family members had disrespected her in the form of old cliche ideas.

"You can't live in your car forever." was one of her favorites, because she always mustered the courage to ask "Why?"

To which, of course, there was never a response. Ha! She *did* have plans.

No, sorry Aunt Nancy, she often thought, *I wasn't planning on living in my van till I was sixty, despite the times you told me I can do whatever my wild feminine heart desires.*

Georgia had hit the automotive jackpot a year earlier when she inherited a 1987 Toyota van from a family member living in Reno.

Her great aunt had explained the situation over the phone one day, that she was moving into retirement housing and to "just come over and get it. I won't use it anymore." All Georgia had to do was fly out, get it looked at by a mechanic, and then drive it on home to California. After an inspection, the guy told her it needed transmission work and a tune to the breaks but, other than that, it would make a drivable vehicle. Georgia saw an opportunity. She felt it beat the cost of rent in Los Angeles to put the work into it, so it was a deal. Install a couple shelving units, buy a mattress, and home sweet home.

Georgia had ideas and expectations from her own future, of course. But for now the name of the game was to save money and see what tomorrow would bring. That was about it. A simple way of life for a seemingly simple gal.

Single and simple, Georgia embodied the classic physicality of a California, bleach-blonde surfer girl. Her wavy yellow hair and Valley girl inflection gave off the impression that she had just spent the morning surfing (which she probably had). Not perfect in the face but knowing how to apply the eye liner in order to draw eyes, she held her posture much grander than a woman of thirty usually might. She liked to think that's what attracted men of a more powerful stature to her.

Not that she cared about men's opinions anyway. Or so she'd have you think.

If you could sum up Georgia's personality in one image it would be that time when her sister walked in on her in their shared, downtown, one-bedroom apartment, about ten years ago.

"What in hell are you doing?" Her sister asked inquisitively, eyeing the girl who had a tape measure pulled up around the circumference of her bosom.

"I'm trying to see if I'm a brick house. I think I'm 34-24-30 though, so whatever." Content and complacent, she kept moving the cloth measuring tool down and up to get her dimensions.

She was almost boringly simple though. Georgia kept to herself more often than not, becoming a sort of shut-in ever since the bad break-up with what's-his-name, just before the serendipitous fate of being offered her van. It's not that she was afraid of putting herself out there, necessarily. She just didn't see a reason why she should. She'd attend the random party but would usually call it a night after a single beer; or she'd just sit around her van watching old cop movies and falling asleep early. She never really felt the itch of loneliness creep up on her. If she was being honest with herself she'd say her real dream was that something wild would fall into her lap. But at the end of the day, Georgia supposed it was better for life to be normal than dramatic. Which was what made it all the more difficult to cope with Isabelle's disappearance and the surfacing of that creepy motherfucker Steve.

-

He arrived at her work one night to "ask a couple questions".

It was about seven o'clock in the dead of winter at the El Segundo all-night diner Georgia worked at. She was on the tail end of a double shift and figured it was the perfect time for a break before cleaning up after the early-bird dinner rush. She was a server at the casual little establishment, spending her days running around in a light blue mini dress and off-white apron, pouring one endless cup of coffee after the other. On their breaks, the servers would sometimes choose to eat what the cooks have pushed aside into the recesses of their greasy kitchens.

It was something that happened often. If a server just so happened to meander back to the kitchen when they were hungry they might scan the counter tops and cutting boards for some scraps, misfires or even partially burnt food. All in the name of starvation. She had stopped Luis and asked him about a botched Caesar salad that sat in the back corner of the kitchen.

"Es not fresh, Georgia. I can make you fresh one." he implored sweetly.

"No, it's totally cool. I'll just take it." She said with a weak smile, not wanting to stir the pot with the cooks any more than when she had to ask for that tuna salad on the fly an hour ago.

So she sat in the back of the depleted diner, eating the slightly wilted concoction of dark green romaine, Parmesan, and, ah, there was the mistake....ranch instead of Caesar dressing. Georgia munched on.

She had just sat down and shoveled in two or three fork-fulls when she saw him walk in the front door. He resembled a dirty gangster from some 1970's sitcom. His swagger was messy and his hair in even more disarray. It was yellow but not pretty or wavy. Darker and shorter, kind of bowled in a disheveled way, looking as if it hadn't been washed in about a month. The only word that came to mind when the girl set eyes on him was "greasy". His black suit was baggy and too big for him. His sleeves hung past his palms and the collar of his dated suit coat lay limp and wrinkled. He wasn't particularly tall but his slightly protruding belly had a couple buttons on his white shirt struggling to keep the contents in. Still, he had a look about him. Despite not being attractive to Georgia he seemed kind of bad-ass. Almost sexy in his general style. Like one of the characters in those noir heist movies she so favored, but definitely not someone she'd hang around with. Like the old drunks who cornered her in the diner whenever she had to work graveyard; they had plenty of stories to share about their elusive, boyish pasts. She always drifted off and pictured the male gorilla, puffing up his chest in order to seem like the best mate in the jungle. Those men never seemed to realize that she didn't want to hear any of it. It was perhaps, in this moment, when Georgia realized "bad-ass" and "appreciated" very rarely went hand in hand.

She chewed as she watched him approach one of the other servers near the entrance. The man in black gestured stoically to the boy, Benny. In his forever weary demeanor, Benny looked up and feigned interest in whatever the man had to say.

It's hard to keep the happy mood when dealing with old fashioned diner patrons who only tip a nickel on a two dollar cup of coffee.

Benny nodded before finding a way to boringly point to the corner where Georgia sat, minding her own business with her little half-eaten salad. She shoved one more big bite in before the guy arrived to her table. Almost as if to say "I don't care that you're coming over here, I have my own things to do right now, bud."

As he got closer she saw him eyeing her up and down with an offensively devious smile. Georgia felt vulnerable just to have his eyes on her. He didn't scare her but she was sure he was up to no good, whoever he was. He held himself meanly, nastily, rudely. When he finally spoke, he sounded more droll than she anticipated.

"Are you Georgia?" he asked her, in a quick, raspy Jersey accent that came off as if he was in a rush to get back to his double parked car.

"Who are you?" She asked as she sat back in her seat, remembering her strict mother's "stranger danger" policy.

"My name is Steve. And, well, do you know a gal named Isabelle?"
Now starting to get worried about who the hell this guy really was, Georgia dropped the water-spotted fork onto her plate and looked at him with a furrowed brow.

"Why, what happened to her, where is she?"

"Calm down, ma'am. We don't know where she is right now. We tried her phone, her brother's place, their parent's…" He held a hand out in an attempt to calm her while the other remained tucked into his pocket. "I just wanted to ask you a couple questions."

Georgia was starting to worry herself, indeed. Isabelle had been her best friend since the two met in middle school and bonded over the same hatred for mathematics class. Isabelle, the rambunctious young beaut, had been known for her rebellious tendencies. She would get pulled out of school-yard fights in high school and move on to get pulled out of bar fights in her twenties. The raven rebel had slowed down quite a bit in the last couple years though. She was notorious for changing the pace of her life and the track she was on. Georgia remembered this time last year when Isabelle was talking about moving to Pennsylvania in attempts to live on some communal farm and become a vegan. Last she heard the girl was working tables at a prestigious Los Angeles night club and living with her brother in Hawthorne, reexamining her desire to become an actress. Isabelle wasn't crazy or even immature. She was very talented and smart and savvy, as a matter of fact. The two had similar ideals on what life should and could be. And Georgia's sisterhood with Isabelle was very important.

"What questions?" Georgia asked defensively, palms flat on the table now.

"When was the last time you saw her?" He asked at once.

"Like a week ago."

"Uh huh." Steve eyed her and became distracted by the strange plate of food that was before her. "What the hell are you eating?" he chuckled lightly and brought up a few fingers to cover his crooked smile in a swaying, half-drunken kind of way.

"Dude!" Georgia said loudly, startling the man and a few patrons a couple booths away. "Well we have to find her, I can go to her place and wait and, hey, I can try to call her!" She got up from her booth and made her way for the back office just beyond the front registers.

"Benny, I'm leaving for the police station, it's an emergency." Benny rolled his eyes and continued on to table seven with two plates of meatloaf.

"No, no, no," Steve said in tow to the woman who was already rushing back from the office with her coat, rifling around in it's pockets for her cell phone. She stopped behind the counter and struggled to put the thing on and search the pockets at the same time.

"That won't be necessary, I already have a guy waiting at her place, and we called her and whatnot. Left tons of messages." He stammered in his Jersey accent and actually tripped on a nearby table while attempting to move toward her, trying to play it cool and putting his hands back in his pockets. Georgia looked at him, slowing down in her tracks a bit. She eyed him up and down, keeping her head straight and becoming suspicious of the circumstances, now. At first she assumed the guy was a cop but it might be prudent to be cautious of the stranger.

"Ma'am, do you know a guy named John Goldman?" Of course Georgia knew John. He was Isabelle's older brother. She spent many a family gathering and uncomfortable party turning down his very eager advances. But she wasn't sure if divulging in details with *Mr. Steve* would warrant any positive outcome. So she answered with a simple "Yes."

"Well, John Goldman is missing right now, too. We really want to speak with him. We believe him to be dangerous. So if you know anything..."

He paused to study her face, squinting and tilting his head to the right.

She looked right into his eyes with the same squint, head tilted to the left.

"...or if you hear anything. You just let me know."

He handed her a piece of paper with the small print of his first name and seven numbers. It wasn't even a business card. Who the hell was this guy? He turned to leave and once he got to the door he paused and turned back to look at her.

"Oh and Georgia?"

She began taking off her coat slowly, looking up at Steve.

"I'll be waiting for your call."

And with that she watched as he darted out the door, letting it slam as he continued down the street and out of view.

Georgia thought quick. Everything seemed out of place. Nothing about this guy appeared genuine at all. She didn't expect herself to come up with such a wild reaction but, in the heat of the moment, she acted quickly. Whatever she did she had to do it fast.

"Benny, I'm leaving."

Benny responded with another dramatic eye roll and watched as Georgia put her coat on again. She found her phone finally, and tucked it back into the side pocket that it came from. Grabbing her keys out of the opposite pocket, Georgia disappeared out the door.

-

Out the door, she continued on the path she saw Steve take. Down a few paces to the right of the entrance there was an alley that dipped around the diner. From that corner she saw the man, about a hundred yards away, where a new street started and the old towne alley cobblestone ended. Georgia watched him get into a banged up old beige Mustang, start her up, and head east toward Gardena. Luckily her van was only about a half block behind his. She ran down the alley and turned right from where Steve was parked. She hopped into her vehicle and took another cue from her seventies vice movies; follow from a few car lengths behind.

So as to stay inconspicuous.

"Answer, God damnit." Georgia said as she held her cell phone up to her ear with one hand and kept steady at the wheel with the other. Isabelle wasn't answering her phone, just as Steve warned.

What the hell am I doing? What are you gonna do once he stops? Georgia thought to herself with a few quick shakes of her head.

But she drove on nonetheless. There were a couple times in her pursuit when the car in between her and Steve's ditched around a corner, leaving her feeling vulnerable and somewhat abandoned. "No, come back." she'd whisper to herself, a little jolt of concern rushing over her. After about ten minutes of following in "hot" pursuit Georgia saw Steve's junker pull into an old, partially gated warehouse parking lot in South Gardena. Sure she had been spotted but feeling like taking the risk, Georgia let the van slowly roll by the lot entrance. *If I haven't been spotted by now then Steve must either be distracted or stupid.*

When she came to the entrance she saw him standing at a stainless steel work door just a few yards to the right of where his beater was parked. He was fidgeting with some keys, the big lug, and dropped them. With a clumsy scratch to his head he picked them up and used them once more to open the door. He entered, shutting the door behind him, not seeming to notice her at all.

Georgia kept driving until she rounded the next block. Pulling off to the side of the road she put the van in park and cut the engine. She grabbed the cell phone she had tossed to the seat beside her and tried to reach Isabelle one more time. No answer. She even dialed John's number. An answer!

"Hello?" his voice asked merrily.

"John, hey, where are..."

"...Hello?" He asked again.

"John?"

"Just kidding! You've reached John, leave your message after the beep thing, thanks."

God, she hated John.

After the beep she left a brief, angry, message for him and shoved the phone back into her pocket. She considered her options.

As of now Georgia knew nothing concerning Isabelle's or John's disappearances. They might just be at some party or just out for a long weekend.

Georgia brooded calmly as she peered out at the starless night sky. It would be the responsible thing to do, she thought, to call up Isabelle's parents. Or even call the police and have them check on everything. But Georgia didn't want to do the responsible thing right now. Something inside her was begging to try something new. She had this nagging feeling that Isabelle was alright wherever she was, causing trouble with her brother, no doubt. Even if they were in trouble, Georgia was feeling impulsive and tired. Tired of simplicity. Tired of sitting still.

So there was only one apparent option left. If Georgia had been any different of a woman, ignorant or more susceptible to the wickedness of the world, then Steve would really seem scary. His masculinity and east-coast confidence was one that west-coasters didn't always know how to handle. But as it stood, she was unnerved. She saw right through that ruffian-wannabe exterior and what she saw was a match. The two were alike, in a sense. Where Steve seemed to act tough on the outside and actually be a simpleton on the inside, she was the opposite. Georgia had the ruffian inside her and she wanted to let it out more than anything. And she intended on getting what she wanted.

So Georgia started up her van and pulled back around the corner she came from. She slowly rolled into the lot and parked to the left of Steve's shitty beige beast. There was light illuminating their vehicles from a drapery-covered window next to the door. Inside she could make out a hefty shadow swaying from one side of the room to the other. Georgia took a deep breath and hopped out of the van, tucking her keys into her jacket pocket as she made her way to the door. She watched as Steve's shadow stopped in it's tracks at the sound of her knock upon the metal.

Please be the only one in there, She thought to herself.

-

Knock knock knock
There was a long pause. Georgia waited maybe thirty seconds. A minute.

Just ditch now, it's not too late, run for it, this is so stupid, you are so stu...
The door flung open and there stood Steve. His face went from confused to stoically scared in an instant before, suddenly, his eyes fell back to normal again; coy-like, as if he didn't want to give off too much information.

But he already had.

"I thought I'd come talk to you more about Isabelle and John." She said plainly and quite successfully faking a tone of concern.

She felt ready. She could fight someone right now. Adrenaline pumped and her mind felt sharp as Japanese steel. Steve hesitated for a moment. He was still wearing that suit coat that was too big for him. He hunched before her, looking Georgia up and down once more, much to her disapproval. She thought about punching him then and there for that alone. She also thought *what the hell is he waiting for?*

After another ten seconds passed he stepped back, opening the door a little wider for her to enter, a revolting grin on his face.

"Yeah. Come on in."

"Thank you." She said politely, making her way for the center of the room, posture in check and hands at her sides. She smiled at him as he shut the door, matching his great big disgusting grin with one of her own. Was this working on him? Or was he playing the same game she was?

"I'll, uh..." Steve stammered a bit as he walked towards the girl, stopping a mere foot away from her. "I'll be right back."

As he walked away he called back to the young woman.

"Have a seat, there, make yourself comfortable. When I come back we'll talk."

Georgia turned to look at the place. It was unclear as to whether Steve was actually living here or not. Despite the fact she lived with the bare minimum herself, Georgia wasn't sure many other people could handle that kind of lifestyle these days.

The room reminded her of her father's old workshop. Dusty with a hint of cigarette smoke, it smelled of nostalgia. It made her feel a little more regal in the moment. There was a table surrounded by a few metal chairs just to her left. An old plaid easy chair sat at the opposite side of the room, across from a 90's model upright TV stand. Behind that, in the south corner of the room, was a large water heater. One large oriental-patterned rug sat underneath most of it, making it seem cozier.

It really tied the whole room together, she thought, attempting to chuckle at herself in the throws of her adrenaline rush. It was a large room, despite the small living quarters. Nick-knacks and clunky furniture pieces were stacked beyond the little living space. Boxes, furniture, tools, and even another clunky car like Steve's could be seen under a cover of plastic and a thin coating of dust in the back. *Does this guy live here? Is it a hideout? Is anyone else here?*

She continued to keep her wits about her.

To the far left beyond the dining set was a little office you could see through a little window, almost completely covered from sight by junk stacked upon junk. That was where Steve disappeared to. Georgia made her way to the table and sat in a scratched up metal chair. The brown seat cushion was cracked and some of the white stuffing was starting to seep out. She was never a posh girl, never one to see issue with ripped furniture. So she sat and waited for the man, making sure her chair was pushed out from the table just enough so that if she needed to make a break for it she'd have ample space and time.

Those seemingly unrealistic little survival tactics that creeped up surprised her.

Steve returned, meandering slowly over to the table, two opened bottles of beer in his hands. There was a lamp that hung down, perfectly covering his face from Georgia's view. He smiled as he looked at his own bottle, falling into another rickety metal chair across the way. He placed the other bottle in front of Georgia. Putting his beer to his lips, he took a large swig, slumping down into his chair, one arm over the back of his seat and the other fiddling with the label on the stout before him.

Georgia watched as he looked down to her beer, then up at her. Down to her beer and then up at her again.

"Good beer, you should try it." He said in his own soft voice. He still sounded like a gargling Jersey bear to

Georgia. She lifted the beer and caught a whiff of it before it got too close to her lips. She couldn't really believe it but she smelled bleach.

In her mind she was doing back flips and front flips and shaking in wild, wild disbelief.

Is he poisoning me? Could this beer just be highly volatile in it's percentage or did Steve actually think that poisoning me like this would work?

Georgia eyed the man as she casually raised the bottle up higher. Pursing her lips together tight, she feigned a few chugs before slamming the cocktail back on the table before her. The glass on metal made a clang that echoed loudly throughout the room.

"Yummy?" He asked with a demure smile that was almost handsome.

"So yummy." She replied with the same demure, sarcastic tone. She kept her poker face intact while wondering what Steve's game was. Before she could get around to asking any of her round-a-bout questions, the man leaned forward and chuckled at her.

"Well I'm glad you liked it, *Parker*." He taunted Georgia, much to her confusion. She furrowed her brow a bit and squinted in response.

"Because now," He leaned back into his chair, confidently. "you're gonna die from that '*yummy*' drink I just concocted for you."

Georgia wasn't quite sure of a proper response. *Die?! He actually just tried to kill me, what the fuck?*

She had to persist and improvise. Conforming to a simple approach and, for the time being ignoring the fact he forgot her name, Georgia played the only hand she figured she had. Figuring Steve to be a simple man of the simplest pleasures, if there was one thing Georgia liked to think she had mastered among her many traits it was the psyche of the simple man.

Thank you Lynerd.

Georgia relaxed her gaze. "How long do I have, Steve?" She asked with a slow, feigned sadness.

"Not too long, toots." He said with his beer to his lips, finishing off the bottle and throwing it into the corner of the room before smiling widely to himself. The sound of the shattering glass startled Georgia but not as much as the loud yowl Steve let out.

"Woo-weee I finally got the bitch!" He then mumbled to himself as he pulled a hidden cigarette from behind his ear and a lighter from his pocket. "And it wasn't even hard. She came right to *me*. Screw Vinnie, he don't know shit." He lit the cigarette and leaned back again, looking at the ceiling in pure delight at his endeavor.

"What the hell a gal like you is doin workin in a shit hole diner like that, tho, I don't get." He cocked his head to the side and continued his upward gaze. "A cover maybe. I dunno."

He really pondered that last part and it distracted him enough to allow Georgia a moment to think.

She was confused but still in improv mode. She continued on with whatever she thought he meant. Had he known Isabelle or John? Did she actually know him? Did he know about her? *Parker?*

"Aww, Steve. You got me." She said, her arms flopped onto the table, throwing her head down upon them, looking up to the idiot through shy eyes, biting her lip.

No aggressive stances, play the injured bird, keep eye contact. Let's see just how vulnerable you are, Steve.

All those lessons that mama taught her about survival at the hands of a mad man would come into play. That ever-told Oprah show household story of the woman who played coy with her intruder until the "right moment" always stayed in the back of Georgia's mind. So the five-foot-seven blonde from suburban Irvine flirted.

"Awwwww" She moaned in her best drunken valley-girl tone. "Well Steve, since it's all gonna end anyway," she continued in the sultriest voice she could muster "why don't you come to my van? I live there." She noticed she had gotten his attention. His cigarette sat burning between his fingers as he looked down his nose at the pretty young thing in his den.

"It's got a bed." She finished with an inflection that had him. Standing from her chair slowly she leaned into him this time, her head narrowly missing the lamp above.

"Please?" And with that he stood. He made his way for the door and held it open. He threw his cigarette outside and looked back to the girl with a charming, dunce-like smile.

"Well then, what are we waitin' for, doll?"

-

Steve followed her out the door and they made their way for Georgia's shining silver beast.

Georgia had some adventurous times in that van and had no regrets living in it. Besides the trouble of finding parking at times, she felt like a goddess in her van. Her neon yellow longboard sat tied tight to the top, like a crown. The front console area was cozy and stocked with most of her essentials, make-up box, laundry basket, etcetera. Behind the front bucket seats was the real living space, however. A cozy nest sat in the back, truly a cave of comfort; curtains, books, battery operated lighting and piles of blankets and pillows. Every time Georgia caught sight of her nest she couldn't wait to curl up and experience the pleasure of rest.

But this time, the happiness that filled her was not due to her bed.

It was the ax she kept handy next to it.

As they got closer to the van Georgia watched Steve from the corner of her eye. She couldn't believe it. Like a well-groomed frat boy that had just been told by some sorority girl "Hey, big boy, let's go back to your place." Steve wore the biggest grin.

He didn't seem like he suspected anything.

Does he really not suspect anything?

So she continued on with her charade.

Georgia choreographed her stunt carefully. But not too carefully, she thought. She'd hate to actually deviate from the simple con that seemed to work so well with this guy. She slowly led him to the right side of the van and feigned a tug at the back sliding door.

"Shoot it's locked. I'll go open it from the other side. You stay right here, *big boy*." She shot him a look to see if he was catching on yet.

Same shit-eating grin. He actually thought he was going to "get some" from a woman he supposedly just killed.

Georgia walked to the other side of the car and opened the opposite sliding door. Of course it was unlocked already. *It's called a key fob, Steve, you ignorant son-of-a-bitch.* She slid it open and hopped inside. Just where it was supposed to be. Her trusty three pound ax. She remembered buying it at the thrift store six months before. Hickory handle and a hand-forged blade with only a few chips, she figured the thing would come in handy and was eager to find a use for it.

Looking up and out the window she saw Steve, standing there with his hands tucked in his pockets, looking up at the night sky, oblivious. She almost felt bad for the guy but ended up easily remembering the situation she was in. She remembered Isabelle and what this guy seemed to know about her. And then she remembered the bleached beer.

Georgia flung the door open.

"Hey, Parker..." Steve said in a sultry voice, only to look into the van and find that his face was soon met by the blunt side of an ax. Georgia felt justified in not giving him the full force of her rage, but, as it stood, she still wanted to punish him for treating her like they might be equals.

Steve fell to the ground and Georgia continued pelting him, only with the blunt side, yelping wildly. Shoulders, stomach, thighs, she was sure she'd broken at least one of his ribs but didn't care. Once she noticed he was out cold with a small patch of blood streaming down his temple at the initial place of impact, she stopped. Fifteen or twenty shots in, Georgia gasped for air, looking down to the deed before her. His body was still, eyes shut. Her hands shook with adrenaline and a single tear of rejuvenation was all she let stream down her face. With a jolt Georgia broke away into the van. Still holding the ax, she rifled around in a box of supplies and soon fished out a single metal spoon. She hurried over to Steve again, straddling over his chest and kneeling down toward his head, holding the spoon under his nose. She let out a small sigh of relief. *Good, the bastard isn't dead.* She thought. Although she wasn't entirely sure of why she *hadn't* just offed the guy who was proud to have poisoned her.

That's right. Why on earth would he have wanted to kill her? Steve was stupid, but he knew what he was doing. Or he thought he did. He had a plan, here. Did he think she was someone else? Parker? And who was Vinnie? Steve had a lot of questions to answer and, by God, he was going to answer them whether he liked it or not.

Georgia threw the spoon and the ax into the van. She rifled through her junk box again and pulled out a long spool of rope she kept for emergencies. Throwing it over her shoulder, she slammed the van door shut and took a look around the parking lot. A still dead night. Not a soul around. She looked down at Steve and reached for his arms. Positioning herself accordingly, she grabbed tightly onto his wrists and used the rest of her adrenaline to drag him back into his pathetic den.

-

About an hour later Georgia finally heard Steve stir. She had been sitting in his plaid easy chair, back in the dirty warehouse, watching over his blacked out body in which she tied securely to his rusty water heater. Georgia attempted to reach Isabelle a couple more times on her phone while she waited. Still no response.

But the woman had set the scene in the warehouse so perfectly, she thought. Tossing the table and chair set about the room, she hoped to give off the impression that a tornado was destroying Steve's life. Georgia even carefully tipped the TV to it's side next to where she tied him up. She was the menace to his society.

"Well well well, how did you sleep, Steve?" Georgia asked very nicely, indeed, approaching the man and crouching down next to his outstretched legs. She had the high ground now, and planned to use it to her advantage. Georgia began second-guessing the effectiveness of her knot tying skills once Steve started fidgeting. She used a good three yards of rope to secure his hands behind the structure and his torso to it's base, but left his feet unbound.

"Hope you don't mind, I fixed the place up a bit." She gestured around the room flamboyantly with her little ax that she had gone back for, looking at Steve with contemptuous crazed humor in her eyes.

The man was just coming to, looking around, readjusting to his surroundings. Once he realized where he was and just what was happening to him his face remolded from confused to petrified in an instant. Quite the chameleon, he was.

"No." Steve mumbled in melodramatic defeat "No. No!" Steve screamed hysterically as the tears started pouring from his swollen eyes. His sobs led to a face shrouded in fear. Drool ran down the sides of his mouth as he sobbed in anger.

"God damn you, Parker! Why aren't you dead?" He screamed almost comically as he shook his head in disbelief, now wiggling about frantically in attempt to loosen himself from his shackles.

"You idiot, I knew you were trying to poison me. I didn't drink your damn beer!" She screamed even louder, flailing her ax around.

"Who just tries to kill someone? What is wrong with you?" Her shouts turned into high pitched shrieks.

"Well you were gonna kill *me,* I had to do something!" He responded as he bowed his head in defeat. "You're gonna kill us all!"

"Alright, Steve." Georgia held her ax up and in Steve's face as she settled into a kneeling position next to him. "It's time for you to answer a few questions." She said. "And if you try to play games with me..." Steve cut her off by throwing a foot in the air and catching her nose with the toe of his boot. Georgia tumbled backward, her ax flying towards the front door as she reached for her face, moaning in disbelief.

"Moron!" Georgia managed to catch her balance and scream through the blood dripping across her lips. She was almost impressed. Steve still trembled as he watched her stumble forward again, lifting her fist and punching him across the left cheek. In one quick moment his head ricocheted off the water heater and whipped back forward.

He screeched and lowered his head in pain. Georgia watched Steve recoil and turned away to evaluate the damage done to her face.

"Oh no." He whimpered as he looked down at this crotch in embarrassment. Georgia turned back to Steve only to catch him in the act of actually pissing his pants. Georgia let her bloody hands fall to her side in astonishment, jaw dropping.

"Jesus, Steve." She said, like a disappointed mother to her two-year-old son who just wet himself at the jungle gym. Georgia gathered herself and remembered why she was there in the first place. She needed to know why this guy was looking for her friend. And whoever this Parker person was, Steve was scared shitless of her. And that was a good place to be in order to get answers.

"Steve, where the fuck is Isabelle?" Georgia was sure to keep her distance from Steve and his flailing feet but felt he was breaking more and more by the second. He sobbed, looking up into her eyes.

"I don't even know." His voice was shaky and alert as he finally gave in. "Last I heard she was in Vegas with that idiot Johnny. He took her there to spend the money he stole from Vinnie." He fumbled for more words, bravely finishing his thought. "We wanted to catch up with her, see how much of our money she was out spending. But then I caught wind that she was friends with *you*. And Vinnie had already decided that he didn't want to do anything about it, which I think was stupid!" He recoiled in slight terror and sat looking like a child. "You maniac!"

Georgia paced about, trying to piece everything together. It sounded like the only person who was a real threat was Steve. Whatever lunatics John was mixed up with, well, they must have figured out that Isabelle wasn't a problem. Hopefully. She chose to ignore the whole "Parker" thing for now. The question remained, where was Isabelle? Georgia began feeling very overwhelmed, until suddenly her phone began ringing from the inside of her jacket pocket. She hurried to pull it out with her bloodied hand only to look at the caller ID. It was Isabelle. Wiping her index finger clean on her pants, she pressed the "Answer" button on the screen.

"Isabelle, where the hell are you?" She almost shouted as she stared off both into space and at Steve, who was now looking at her with wide, curious eyes.

"I'm at John's, why? Are you ok?" Georgia plopped herself back into Steve's easy chair and let out a sigh of relief. "I'm sorry, G, my phone was dead and I just got back here to plug it in. John and I went to Vegas!" Isabelle was her regular excitable self and Georgia responded in her usual mom voice.

"Isabelle, listen to me, I think John's in some kind of trouble..."

Isabelle giggled. "Yeah no shit, he got arrested on the strip." Georgia was inconsolably shocked.

"So it's true, he stole money from some gangsters?"

"What?" Isabelle mumbled distractedly. "No, where did you hear that?"

Georgia was silent as her continued gaze at Steve changed from worried to innocently confused.

Steve still stared back like a deer in the headlights. Isabelle continued on.

"No, so John came home yesterday and was all bummed cause his work fired him. I felt bad, so I decided to take some of the money our parent's just sent me and drive us up to Vegas for a night. When we got there John started getting drunk and obnoxious, taking his clothes off and yelling at the drag queens, the ones you can take pictures with, you know who I'm talking about?"

Georgia simply nodded and waited for the girl to go on.

"Well anyways, that's when I found out that John was on speed."

Georgia rolled her eyes and nodded to Steve.

Deer in the headlights.

"The cops come up while he's running around in his boxers singing Christmas carols. An hour later I go bail him out and drive us home and that's the story of why I hate my brother." Isabelle trailed off with another feminine giggle and waited for Georgia's response.

Georgia recoiled and rolled her eyes again. She hated John.

Steve just sat watching Georgia's face, damp and still tied firmly to the water heater, making no attempt to escape it's clutches.

"You should come over and watch a double feature with me! John went to spend the night at Monique's place and I'm all alone here."

Georgia considered what to do about Steve.

"G? You still with me?"

"Sorry, Izzy!" Georgia snapped back to reality. Happy her friend was alright, she stood and switched her attention from Steve to the girl on the other end of the receiver.

"I'll be over in a bit, ok?"

"Bring tacos!" And with that Georgia hung up her phone, shoving it back into her pocket.

She looked over to Steve who was already shaking his head vigorously.

"Nuh uh, you ain't goin anywhere, Parker."
Georgia squinted at him inquisitively.

"Steve, are you serious? You still think I'm...?"

She was interrupted when the front door of the warehouse flew open. It was a man, short and well dressed, donning a silky blue neck tie beneath a silver sport jacket and over a black shirt. His small but stout stature should have made him look less threatening but it didn't. Piercing green eyes and meticulously greased chestnut hair, he held himself like a man who had come into a good amount of money over night, but had a face that suggested the money he made might be useful when it came to convincing people he meant business.

"Steve, where have you been all day? And what the hell's goin' on here?" The man had a Jersey accent to match Steve's. Barely giving Georgia a glance, let alone the time of day, she lifted a hand to her nose again when she felt more blood drip over her lips. The man placed his fists on his hips, moving his jacket back away from his belly, revealing a holster that contained a massive silver pistol. So why wasn't he just shooting her, Georgia wondered. She clearly had his man in a very undesirable position.

"Vinnie I got Parker! I got her, boss." Steve was near out of breath with relief.
They both looked at Steve before Vinnie turned to look at Georgia, who felt obliged to remove her hand from her face so Vinnie could see that she was not, in fact, "Parker". Vinnie shook his head and walked towards the soaked man, crouching down in front of him and eyeing the ropes.

"Steve what are you talkin' about? This broad ain't Parker." He started chuckling at Steve's expense. "Besides, if this is you capturing someone, Steve, I think you're doing it all wrong." He shot an unimpressed papa bear glance at Georgia. "What the hell made you think this was Parker anyways?" He asked as he began looking for a way to untie Steve, resorting to pulling a short switch-blade out of his jacket and hacking away at the braids. Georgia flinched at the sound of the ropes being cut loose and, spotting her ax near her feet, bent over slowly to pick it up.

"The guys said that John's sister was friends with Parker, so we needed to tread lightly. I was trying to take care of it, boss."

Vinnie stood once he freed Steve of his ropes and pointed at Georgia.

"They said I couldn't take someone like Parker out but I knew I could, boss."

"You stupid idiot, you think a deadly Greek assassin is hangin around Ingelwood?" He eyed her up and down, cringing at the sight of the blood from her nose, which had now run down to the front of her coat. "Those guys were screwing with you! Stupid jerk. If *that* was Parker, you'd be dead by now."

"Well he almost was, for what he put me through!" Georgia waved her ax towards Steve like a mad woman and looked to Vinnie for some semblance of justice. Steve remained seated, rubbing his sore, red wrists.

"I just wanted to help." Interrupted Steve in a whisper.

"Besides, she works in the east!" Vinnie continued on, ignoring Steve's little plea.

"People move all the time." Georgia offered sarcastically as she looked to Vinnie, who was not, as it turned out, interested in her opinion *or* granting her anything more than a ticket to freedom.

"Who the fuck are you?" He finally asked her, put out by her presence. While she wondered how to answer that, Vinnie broke the silence.

"Get outta here!"

And with that Georgia bolted towards the door, ax in tow. As she left the warehouse and shut the door she heard Vinnie chastise his little henchman.

"What am I gonna do with you, Steve, you worthless little shit?"

-

Georgia got back to her van, hopped in, and locked the doors. She sat for a minute, really going over the events that just took place. She twisted the rear view mirror towards her and studied her bloody reflection. The nose had stopped dripping. And it didn't feel broken, she thought. "Deadly assassin." She chuckled to herself as she grabbed her keys, started her van, and drove North for Hawthorne.

Dead Cottage
Entry one

The impending doom revolving around the new "infection-caused" apocalypse wasn't the scariest part to me. Mostly it was that everyone was immediately calling it the "zombie apocalypse" which just felt so knee-jerk. So tinsel. So kitsch.

I was blasé to the whole ordeal.

It also happened to be the rickety old inn that they were ushering us into on the island that late afternoon that really pissed me off.

Our Western Canadian island was one of true granola population. Tree huggers on the path to enlightenment. They lived in this semi-reclusive haven in a plethora of classes; in tents and yurts on someone's back acreage, or else in a mansion in the mountains, only coming down to stock up on cases of unsweetened almond milk.

No neon lights, no traffic lights. No big-box outlets and no darkened alleys with oily dumpsters ripe for the loitering. I didn't always feel like I was a part of their "good ol days" ways, attending the local seed bank clubs and listening to their acoustic bluegrass jams at the open-mic nights, but here I lived.

It might have been the feeling that I was a survivor on the island. I didn't have to worry about the city mainland fast-food-world bullshit or actually smelling really good after a day of kayaking. It was fun to leave my house and play on survival mode. Trail running in the woods and challenging my distance, or collecting herbs and studying their healing properties. Throwing knives at makeshift bulls-eyes on logs at the beach was always my favorite. I was teaching myself solid life skills here. It felt hardcore as hell.

So no, holing myself up in a shack when shit was supposedly hitting the fan wasn't about to happen. Because, man, once the news got around and they gathered a bunch of us up to take shelter in that field just outside of town I was livid. The cynical, centrist, realist commoner in me was kind of fed up by all the negligent, blind fear in the eyes of the once spiritually awakened.

I don't know how it started because, no, I didn't ever look into it, or buy into the fear mongering. Perhaps I should have. Something about a particular bruise or wound that was making its way from host to host, I guess. There seemed to be only one or two cases of an extreme "turn" that any of us even heard about. Everyone just started quoting these articles from the Times and I was like "Well, that paper's super biased, anyways. Did you research it?"

No one ever researches.

None-the-less we were about to be ushered, single file, into a twenty-room motel that, I'm pretty sure, was built in the 1800's by a guy that didn't know his mortar from his bricks.

Which wouldn't matter anyways because the whole thing was built from crusty wood and rusted nails.

Myself and the group, smelling like a collective puddle of sweat from an armpit that hadn't seen a conventional deodorant in years, made our way in and up the spiral staircase from the front entrance.

The first floor was small and the whole building was round. It was probably about thirty paces from the front doors to the opposite side of the room and the only things to look at were a small side table by the entrance and that creaky set of stairs; both made of the same wood used to construct the dilapidated shelter, I'm sure. The house seemed to move each time someone's feet touched a step, which was about every half-second. There was about thirty of us, seeming like so many more in this small space.

One woman at the tail end of the group kept screaming out, trying to organize the bodies into bedrooms. She held a massive white board in her arms, quite impressively, as a matter of fact.

She shouted out numbers and was met with the shouts of names.

People shouted numbers back, to which she would reply with a shouted out name to that number.

She wrote the names and numbers on her board and looked down at her work with much aplomb before continuing on with her duties. This continued on for a time while she kept praising everyone for their orderliness in this "trying time".

I figured old habits die hard, despite there being a supposed populous epidemic that could wipe the human race from existence. It was Mavis's (or Mary's or Martha's or Mabel's, I don't recall) time to shine in the eleventh hour.

I moved on.

There were a good amount of bedrooms in this ten story shed, much to my doubt.

I looked around the place as if searching for the answers to my many questions. Why do I hear so much giggling, like we're all at a slumber party? Why is everyone concerned with a bedroom right now? Where's all that walking death I heard so much about? And is this the best emergency evacuation setting this "civilized" island has to offer? I guess most people left on that last ferry out this morning when they read whatever it was they read and heard whatever they heard. We were most of what was left in town that afternoon.

Anyway, the woman organizer was still walking about and shouting as we climbed those spiral stairs.

Up the steps I continued, still in slight shock at people's demeanor despite it all. Suddenly I realized the shouting from Miss Organizational-Skills had died down and there were no more people shouting back to her. I had absentmindedly made it to the eighth floor when I realized I hadn't heard my name called. I turned back down to find the board with everyone's names and numbers written on it. It hung on the wall near the front door.

I don't remember being written down, or screaming a name or a number or having a number screamed at me.

But there I was; fifth row down, three columns over:

Room 19   India

I turned and looked back up the stairs while I thought again.

Room nineteen...four rooms per story, not counting the first floor...sixth. Sixth floor? This place is so rickety, what if the seventh, eighth, ninth, and tenth floors crumble down on me in my sleep? Better yet, what if I crumbled down on the fifth, fourth, third, and second floors? I suppose I could try to make it to a door frame or bath tub in time...

What an existence this is. What is life right now, anyways?

I turned to the front door. This is beyond the pale, the way these people want to live. I know I've never truly got along well with them, but this? They were already up there braiding each others hair and strumming peace ballads on their untuned Epiphones. Ratty magazine cutouts of Jimi and Bob were already being pinned to walls and, oh good, now I smell pot! Glad everyone is so relaxed.

What is everyone waiting for and what do they think this is?

I'd make it further on my own. Besides, I have to see what's going on out there. Who's alive, who's dead? Is there really a plague? Probably not, the poor sheep.

Making my way out the door I followed the long path beyond the overgrown green grass to my car. Opening the door and turning the ignition I began weaving my way through the parked cars (damn Prius's) and made my way for town where I'd hopefully find a newspaper and some internet data to find out what's going on.

I sighed as I approached town, remembering that everyone had closed their shops and, because the ferry services stopped running this morning, there was no newspaper delivery.

I sighed once more when I remembered I had cut my phone service a week earlier in order to assimilate to island life.

And I sighed one final time when I hopped out of my car in a deserted town just to sit on the curb, look over, and see a frothing cripple wobbling towards me muttering something about "brains".

It dawned on me what life was suddenly all about as I slumped into my car and drove back down to the derelict shack that I now call home.

New Friends

It was 3 AM on a Tuesday when Lidia first saw that cockroach crawling up her wall.
She had just moved into her slum of a cheap apartment on Grand Avenue the day before. Her few boxes mostly unpacked, she was sitting on her couch watching a movie, trying to get to sleep, when there it appeared – it wasn't very large, it wasn't too small. It was just a cockroach. A little cockroach, right on the wall, just beyond her television. But why was it crawling up the wall? Standing and approaching, in order to get a good sense of the thing, Lidia cocked her head to the right as she stared daggers at it. Then she swiftly tilted her head to the left as she began considering it's source. Looking down, Lidia's eyes followed the carpet lined by the wall to the left. Nothing inconspicuous. She followed it on down to the right, now. Same old nothing. Turning around, she scanned her home for the best killing material. Ah. A dirty napkin from last

night's pizza. Lidia grabbed it but, when she turned back around to take care of business, the mini beast was gone. Her head darted every which way, this and that, on the hunt for the cockroach. It was nowhere. Lidia spent a solid minute in her insomnia ridden walking coma thinking of where the darn thing could have gone. Finally deciding it was a problem for another day, Lidia turned back to her couch, adjusted away from the spring stabbing her in the back, and soon faded into slumber right as her film had ended and the sun started coming up.

On Wednesday Lidia sprung from her couch around 9 AM. Her alarm hadn't gone off, she lamented to herself. Out the door and on the run, Lidia put in a good days worth of work before getting back to her slum of a cheap apartment on Grand Avenue. Lidia fell asleep on her couch again, this time while she tried to decide what movie to watch.. Promptly at 3 AM Lidia shot awake from a bad dream. Gasping and wheezing, Lidia sat and recollected the dream she just had. "Terrible. Terrible." Was all she could manage to say to anyone who would listen as she just sat and recollected.

Feeling prompted, suddenly, to examine the wall by the TV that she felt inclined to examine the night before, Lidia looked up and saw a familiar face. It was the average little cockroach. But this time it wasn't on the wall. It was on the TV, sitting proper, right in the middle of the screen. Lidia was confused but sat staring at the thing for a few minutes with a nice blank stare. It was as still as she was, as if waiting for her to make a move. Out the corner of her eye, Lidia saw the white sparkle of the napkin she had tried to utilize last night. She reached for it, keeping her eye on the bugger, but let her eyes slip off of it for a brief moment. Much to Lidia's surprise, when she reverted her attention back to the television, it was gone.

With a huff and a puff, Lidia grunted softly and inspected the room around her.

"Why," Lidia lamented to herself as she caressed her own body, "if I didn't know any better I'd think that cockroach is trying to get at me."

No, no, she thought. No, no.

And with that Lidia made her way for her bed, set her alarm, and lay still for a good couple more hours before slumber finally took her.

On Thursday Lidia awoke late again, much to her chagrin. Soon realizing it was her day off, she headed out for errands and laughter. After a full day of fun Lidia arrived home with a friend. Derek was a boy of similar tastes and good company for Lidia. They decided to watch a film together and take in some culture.

"I can't wait to take in some of this culture." Derek expressed boisterously to his friend Lidia.

So Lidia made a little popcorn while Derek fidgeted with the VCR. When Lidia appeared back into the living room, that's when she spotted it. The cockroach was on the couch, sitting very friendly-like next to her good friend Derek.

Lidia screamed and pointed at the couch next to Derek, which scared him enough to make him jump from his seat and shake all over.

In all the commotion, Lidia had taken her eyes off the cockroach and it had, of course, disappeared without a trace. She looked high and low, under and over, all while Derek pointed and laughed at his scaredy-cat friend.

Lidia eventually found the nerve to sit down with Derek and watch the movie, but every now and again she'd find it necessary to check beside, above, and around her for the cockroach she wasn't quite ready to call friend.

It was Friday now and Lidia was sitting around her house. The TV wasn't on, she was watching no movie. There was no fun to be had on this day, and there was no where important enough to be.

Lidia was tired, for she hadn't slept since Wednesday. She couldn't help but think that the cockroach was there. Where? She checked for holes in the floors and along the walls.

Nothing.

She checked under the couch and besides the tables. Still no luck.

Maybe doing the laundry would help flush him away. Maybe some pest control products would do the trick. Perhaps burning the entire apartment down...

Lidia sat on her couch, very frightened, indeed. Staying perfectly still, Lidia thought she heard something.

"It must be you, where are you now, cockroach bug?" Lidia whispered to the room.

A light rustling.

A mysterious bustling.

An oh so quiet, far off chuckling.

"Lidia, I thought you'd be happy to have a friend!" Lidia heard a voice whisper. She jumped up, screamed, and began clawing at her ears in distress. She clawed and clawed to no avail as the coy little voice continued to pester. "I thought we were watching a movie tonight, friend." Said the cockroach. Lidia's fingers were now covered in blood, under her nails were the fast-growing collection of skin and hair that she plucked from her own head. She continued to look high, low, down, around, but couldn't find her friend.

Screams mixed with jovial questionable questions as Lidia fell into the kitchen and began violently opening drawers until she found what she was after.

A little knife, no longer than her hand and no heavier than her self-control.

"Lidia don't hurt me, please!" The high-pitched little voice whimpered as Lidia plunged the knife into her ear, past the drum, and quite a ways through her skull.
The voice of the cockroach stopped.

A feat I'm sure Lidia would be quite proud of.

www.ingramcontent.com/pod-product-compliance
Lightning Source LLC
Chambersburg PA
CBHW050911120626
46552CB00004B/1516